the
Recognition

the Recognition

SILENCING *the* SECRET
COMPANION *of* SELF-LOATHING

PAULA MASTERS

FARMHOUSE PRESS

THE RECOGNITION: SILENCING THE SECRET COMPANION
OF SELF-LOATHING

Copyright © 2025 Paula Masters

All rights reserved

The Recognition is a work of fiction. Names, characters, places, and incidents are products of the author's imagination or used fictitiously. Any resemblance to actual events, locales, or persons, living or dead, is entirely coincidental.

Unless otherwise indicated, Scriptures are taken from The Holy Bible, New International Version®, NIV®. Copyright © 1973, 1978, 1984, 2011 by Biblica, Inc. Used by permission of Zondervan. All rights reserved worldwide. www.zondervan. com. The "NIV" and "New International Version" are trademarks registered in the United States Patent and Trademark Office by Biblica, Inc.

Scripture quotations marked ESV are from The ESV® Bible (The Holy Bible, English Standard Version®), © 2001 by Crossway, a publishing ministry of Good News Publishers. Used by permission. All rights reserved.

Capitalization has occasionally been modified from the original.

ISBN 978-1-7377427-9-1

Published by Farmhouse Press

CONTENTS

1 Noel 1

Part 2 (Noel's emotions) 11

Part 3 (The lens of love) 18

2 John 25

Part 2 (John's emotions) 30

Part 3 (The lens of faith-direction) 35

3 Holly 41

Part 2 (Holly's emotions) 47

Part 3 (The lens of spiritual pursuit) 53

4 Steve 59

Part 2 (Steve's emotions) 64

Part 3 (The lens of truth) 70

5 Jan 77

Part 2 (Jan's emotions) 83

Part 3 (The lens of mercy) 88

6 Noel, John, Holly, Steve & Jan 95

Part 2 (Emotions of change) 101

Part 3 (The lens of patience) 106

1

Noel

Noel heard the chime of an incoming text. She picked up her cell phone and read, "Hi Noel, this is Jan Foley."

Jan is a fellow student at the university. She is confident, fashionable, and, quite honestly, gorgeous. Jan's power to turn heads while walking the campus halls is well known. Other than this, Noel barely knows her.

How did she get my number?

Curious, Noel opened the text to read the remainder of the message: "John gave me your cell number. I hope you don't mind."

John? Has John been hanging out with Jan? Thinking about this possibility unnerved Noel.

Noel and John are close. They share a class with

Jan. The difference is that Noel and John spend study time together outside the college, at bistros, cafés, and trendy eateries. Pairing academics with culinary-infused ambiance has become "their thing." Over time, John has introduced Noel to all sorts of flavors, textures, and gourmet specialties.

A full semester has progressed their friendship. Lately, Noel has been sensing a shift in their connection—something more than just friendship.

Noel typed.

"What can I help with, Jan?"

Although Noel wrote these words to sound casual— her stomach dropped as she pushed the Send button.

Noel watched the dots flicker as Jan began formulating a response.

Anxiety mounted with the unknowns of Jan's impending answer.

Finally, the text came through.

"I missed Tuesday's class. John told me you might have some notes."

Noel remembered that John was absent also that day and began to agonize—*Is this a coincidence? Were John and Jan together?*

Insecurity swept over Noel, and it was huge.

Over the years insecurity had interfered with Noel's otherwise guarded confidence. Noel worked hard at being strong. It helped her reach desired goals. And right now, her education was the objective. Nevertheless, the

Achilles' heel of insecurity ushered in a stream of self-deprecation—*I'm not captivating like Jan or as trendy and self-assured. Why would John choose me?* and so on.

The inner turmoil Noel was experiencing morphed into self-loathing as the hours went by. Even with all Noel's wonderful qualities she did not like some parts of herself, and those feelings overshadowed her confidence. No matter how untrue, she could not shake off these toxic thoughts.

❧

Although Noel passed her notes on to Jan the next day, self-preservation kicked in, as it always did, and it manifested as detachment. She did not express any of her insecure feelings to either John or Jan. This was Noel's self-protection mode—she put up a solid appearance of confidence, and it served her well. Looking at her, no one would ever know how rattled she truly felt.

It did, however, affect her behavior toward John. The next time John texted Noel for a study get-together, she did not respond. She was cold toward him. Without knowing John's heart or any of the details behind Jan's text, Noel assumed John was leading both her and Jan on, and she did not want to be in a competition with Jan.

Jan can have him; I'm not going to even try, she told herself.

After John's many attempts to connect, Noel finally sent him a text letting him know she had decided to take school more seriously and study on her own.

John, feeling powerless, eventually gave up. In time he found a new study partner—Steve, from another class.

❧

Coincidentally, Steve was a friend of Noel's who lived next door growing up. Noel and Steve were close as children—playing kickball, climbing trees, having snowball fights, etc. They had gone their own way in college even though they were at the same university.

When Christmas break finally arrived, Noel couldn't have been more relieved to be out on the open highway traveling home. Blasting her favorite playlist, she cracked open the window and let the chilled fresh air fill the car. The ride was invigorating.

Noel's parents stood on the front porch, beaming as she drove up the driveway. When Noel stepped out of the vehicle, she was hit square on by a giant snowball. Turning to see where it came from, she saw Steve. He stood laughing as Noel quickly knelt to shape her own powdery missile. Soon they were all embracing in holiday hugs.

Later that week, Steve and Noel went for a walk to reconnect and reminisce. Shortly into their conversation, Steve faced Noel and asked, "What happened?"

"With what?" Noel responded.

"With you and John Ryan?"

"John? How do you know John?" Noel was confused by Steve's question.

Noel had distanced herself so much from John, even avoiding the coffee shops they frequented, that she had no idea Steve even knew him.

Noel's friendship with Steve had always been easy. He had been her hero, sticking up for her against menacing neighborhood kids. When Steve was around, she didn't struggle with thinking negatively about herself. Steve felt safe; she trusted him.

"John and I are in the same psych class," Steve answered. "I don't know if you know this, but John was madly in love with you."

Noel's eyes grew wide. She felt her pulse rate and breathing increase.

Am I having a panic attack? The conversation felt surreal, as if she were outside it, watching it. It took her a moment to calm down.

Finally, in a trembling voice Noel spoke. "I was convinced John had feelings for Jan Foley."

"Not at all!" Steve said. "Yes, Jan was after him, but John only had eyes for you."

Steve went on to share how baffled and hurt John was. Tears filled Noel's eyes as Steve relayed how John moved forward and began dating a lovely girl named Holly.

"The truth is, Noel, that as much as John loved you, he eventually realized he could not live in fear of being frozen out with no explanations."

Noel, filled with shock and regret, relayed to Steve the process that had happened in her heart. Time seemed to stand still as they sat on a park bench and talked for hours.

As she recounted the details, Steve began to discern indications of self-loathing that may have led Noel to self-sabotage. He listened closely and couldn't help but be concerned that Noel's negative thoughts about herself drove a faulty narrative, which became self-fulfilling. She lost John as she feared, but it was not to Jan as she had imagined.

"Noel, I think something deeper is going on here," Steve said gently.

"What do you mean?"

Steve used caution with his words because he knew Noel's heart was already hurting. "Would you be open to seeing a counselor?"

"Why?" Noel could sense that Steve was holding back.

"From what you have shared, I think self-loathing may be a challenge in your life."

Noel was quiet for a moment, then spoke. "What do you mean by self-loathing?"

Steve explained in detail that self-loathing was pervasive negative self-perception that involves a lot of self-criticism—much like what she had just freshly conveyed.

Although Steve's words hit hard, a verse in Proverbs came to Noel's mind, "Wounds from a friend can be trusted." *Steve is this kind of friend*, she thought to herself. Noel knew she needed to consider the possibility that self-loathing might be a problem.

Steve recommended a good counselor, a Christian friend he knew personally and who specialized in self-esteem.

Noel wasted no time setting up an online appointment during Christmas break. She desperately wanted to understand why this hijacking of confidence came over her so powerfully—and this time at such a great loss.

Noel looked for a quiet and private space in her parents' house to set up her laptop for a Zoom meeting with her new counselor. She took a deep breath and waited for her call. Finally, the computer rang.

Within minutes of the meeting, Noel could tell she would like this counselor. She was transparent and relatable.

"We all struggle with self-loathing on some level," the counselor stated. These were good signs in Noel's mind—*She is treating me like a person, not just a patient.*

But Noel really knew the counselor was a good fit when she emphasized the part faith has in the process of healing from self-loathing. This felt right to Noel, who came from a Christian upbringing.

The counselor began the session by gently inquiring into Noel's faith background.

"Noel, what role did church culture play in shaping your thoughts about life, and particularly yourself?"

Noel paused for a few moments trying to think back.

Finally, Noel spoke. "To be honest, I remember feeling a lot of shame." She could remember trusted Bible teachers who taught that she (and humanity as a whole) should think of themselves as worthless and insignificant before a holy God.

"We may be onto part of the problem," the counselor interjected. "Religious shaming counteracts the ability to have a healthy sense of self."

Noel had never considered this possibility before.

"Church should be a sanctuary for those who don't feel valued. But when the hurting find themselves submerged in church-wounding theologies of self-deprecation, the *self* part of the soul doesn't feel safe at the very place that should be the safest." The counselor paused, and Noel took a deep breath and let it out as if this realization was monumental. "Keep in mind," the counselor added, "that a relationship with a church is different from a relationship with God."

Noel's heart was moved by the idea that being a Christian didn't mean having the mentality of a doormat. It was a refreshing thought. Noel began to get excited about the idea of getting to know God in a personal way, outside of what was commonly promoted in Christian culture.

To further help Noel take religious guilt off her shoulders, the counselor reframed Noel's perception of a Scripture verse that had often thrust her into self-deprecation mode. It was Philippians 2:3.

"Let's consider the verse together," the counselor suggested.

Do nothing out of selfish ambition or vain conceit. Rather, in humility value others above yourselves.

"Most people interpret this as a directive to disregard themselves and to think they are *not as important* as another person," the counselor stated.

"That's what I've always thought," Noel said.

The counselor continued, "But this kind of thinking leaves the psyche void of personal value—a value God has already told us we have. Naturally, people who struggle with self-image slip into this mindset easily."

Noel related instantly.

The counselor then shared how the following phrase—*Do nothing out of selfish ambition or vain conceit*—was a warning about the susceptibility to self-ambition, pridefulness—and even legalism. "People with these characteristics are prone to think highly of themselves and lesser of others. This means it is 'prideful propensity' that is being redirected in this verse."

Noel began to see that Philippians 2:3 is meant to bring a sense of mutuality of value instead of superiority to the prideful or inferiority to those who felt inferior, like her.

Finally, the counselor asked Noel to consider the last part of the verse—*rather, in humility value others above yourselves.*

This was always the part that tripped Noel up.

The counselor pulled her Strong's dictionary off her shelf and showed Noel that the word *others* means "one another" and "mutuality"—and the word *yourselves* means *the agent and the person acted on are the same.*

"In other words," the counselor asserted, "this verse calls the high-minded person to lift the other 'above' self-vanity to a place of equal value. As far as God is concerned, *the agent and the person acted on are the same.*"

Noel recognized something very special that day. As Christians, we have an opportunity to value people who are perhaps not treated with dignity. Since vain conceit often appears as if it has greater worth, this verse is a stunning neutralization of superficiality and regards everyone equally, including Noel.

PART 2

(Noel's emotions)

Noel felt very comfortable with her new counselor and was looking forward to the next Zoom meeting. Noel thought deeply about the things she had learned in the first session. This time she decided to have a journal to write in. She even bought different color pens for specific topics. For instance, she would use orange for eye-opening thoughts, blue for points that hit home, and green for helpful instruction.

Noel was ready for her meeting.

"Understanding the emotional process of self-loathing will help you identify potential problems in the future when they surface," the counselor said.

Noel was listening carefully.

"From our last conversation I noted a few emotions that we can begin to recognize as they surface."

Noel got out her blue pen.

"In your struggle with John there was an initial agonizing. Do you remember *agonizing* over the different possibilities of what Jan's text might have meant?"

"Yes, I do," Noel said.

"This is what spurred on feelings of *insecurity*, of not being good enough. One emotion fell on the next, leading to an avalanche of self-sabotage," the counselor shared.

Noel underlined the words *agonizing* and *insecurity*.

The counselor pointed out that even though these emotions were different, they were the same in a significant way—each inspired reaction, and together they ignited a big one. This explained why Noel felt like her emotions had been hijacked. It was an emotional overload, and it had taken over.

"I recognized the pattern of insecurity in me when I was talking to Steve about why my heart shut off to John. To be honest, I had not thought in these terms before," Noel said.

The counselor listened, nodding in acknowledgment.

Noel added, "I think it was the loss of John that opened my eyes."

"Grief often works this way," the counselor replied gently. "While loss is heart-wrenching, so often it is what God uses to help us recognize something He wants us to see. Grief brings clarity."

As Noel surveyed her past, she could remember how feelings of insecurity intensified at certain times. For instance, when she was little, the neighborhood girls, annoyed with her big personality, looked for opportunities to shame and embarrass her.

The boys, on the other hand, thought Noel was fun. They enjoyed her energetic enthusiasm. The girls, being jealous, would try to undermine the boys' view. And even though Steve was one of those boys, he never fell for the girls' ploys against Noel. This is the reason Noel had always found solace in Steve.

Nevertheless, the trauma of shaming had already stamped its path in the neural tracts of Noel's mind.

The counselor shared with Noel how trauma, big or small, is stored in the limbic section of the brain. "The limbic is the emotional section of the brain. This explains why a wound from long ago resurfaced with such present intensity, Noel. It emerged fresh from the storage bank inside your brain."

"All of us carry trauma that surfaces with certain associations," the counselor continued. "For you, your lively personality is a traumatic association."

"I never thought of it that way because it felt like shame, not trauma," Noel said.

"Yes, and because you never recognized it as trauma, your efforts always went toward hiding rather than healing," the counselor added. "Of course, not all self-loathing comes from trauma association. Sometimes we simply don't like certain things about ourselves."

Noel used her orange pen to write these thoughts down—they were eye-opening!

Unfortunately, over the years Noel internalized the quality of a sunny disposition in herself as naive, corny, and embarrassing, so she worked hard at hiding it. This resulted in an appearance of being reserved. She hated being bubbly (although it would often sneak out when she was with John anyway). She lived in fear of being made fun of. When her enthusiasm surfaced, she would criticize herself and try to hide it or dismiss it. She didn't *like* it—at all. Deep down inside, Noel was dissatisfied with the way God had made her when it came to this part of her personality.

The counselor shared another verse, asking Noel to write it on a piece of paper to take back with her to the university to think about.

It was Hebrews 12:1 (ESV): "*Lay aside every weight, and sin which clings so closely.*" "The words *every weight* mean a 'mass' or 'bulging load,' " the counselor shared. "Notice that there is a distinction between the words *every weight* and *sin*. Not every weight is labeled sin; it can also be something burdensome like self-loathing."

The counselor gave Noel several other examples of weight to consider:

Insecurity	Fear
Shame	Anxiety
The need for	Depression
reassurance	Performance
Perfectionism	People-pleasing
Obsession	Fixing
Regret	Control

These words—particularly shame and insecurity—gave Noel a picture of what the overload inside her looked like: weighty and debilitating. It certainly felt that way.

"We all share the experience of carrying a mass or bulging load upon our hearts at times. And when this bulging load of feelings overwhelms us—it prompts us to react," the counselor said. She continued, "For each of us the reaction is different. Some people fret, others hide, some try to numb the emotions involved, while others cling, ruminate, lash out, etcetera."

Noel pulled out her green pen for this one. She was writing notes as fast as she could, taking every word of her counselor to heart. "Hang on . . . ," Noel said, "some people fret, others hide, some try to numb the emotions involved, while others cling, ruminate, lash out . . . okay, go ahead."

The counselor continued describing self-loathing in terms of a progressing storm. "The weightiness of emotion churns self-loathing, acting like a pressurized storm system, causing a reaction."

In Noel's case, she feared Jan would win John over. But instead of the typical reaction of possessiveness that commonly accompanies this sentiment, Noel's insecurity drove her to aloofness. The feelings surrounding Noel's overload of the emotion led to *coldness* and *detachment*, almost like the stillness at the center of a tornado. Although catastrophic winds of emotion swirled in Noel's heart, the dead-stillness of the center landed on John.

"Here's the thing," Noel's counselor explained, "because life is filled with brokenness, there will always be the propensity for difficult or heavy emotions." She leaned into the Zoom screen to see if Noel was tracking. "We can't get around the fact that life is filled with troubles. But we can learn how to take the power away from a sabotaging emotion by turning the tables with a new pattern of thought." The counselor paused, again looking to see if Noel was still following. She waited for Noel to lift her head from taking notes.

"How does this happen?" Noel asked.

"We do this by allowing an inflated emotion to serve as an internal alert system," the counselor replied. "We let the intensity of the feeling itself alert us."

The counselor paused and continued. "Think about it this way. The intensity of a fire alarm is a call for safety, right?" Noel nodded. "In the same way, the intensity of an emotion can be the alarm that alerts you to find safety from impending self-loathing."

Noel liked this thought. It felt empowering.

The counselor drove this point even further by suggesting mental imagery. "Begin to become aware when a potency of emotion is present. This built-in alert (intensity of an emotion) becomes a valuable reminder that the emotion or feeling is trying to take control. Every time you feel a rise in emotion, imagine a flashing yellow warning sign that says: 'Danger of self-loathing.' "

Noel was able to visualize this.

When Noel went back to campus, the image of a flashing yellow warning sign made a difference. For instance, during class the professor shared an amusing anecdote that caused Noel to chuckle out loud, but she immediately began to shrink in shame at the thought of looking silly. This familiar but "intense" feeling of shame instantly alerted her and reminded her of the counselor's words, *danger of self-loathing*.

Noel paused and prayed quietly, asking God to help her be brave enough to be herself. And not just this, but to also value the way God had created her. Her burst of laughter was a unique personality trait that inspired joy. Shame had been wrongly placed for many years on this endearing characteristic. This was the beginning of Noel getting to know how lovingly God had created her and learning to like who that is.

PART 3

(The lens of love)

Back on campus, Noel was curled up with a warm cup of tea in her dorm room, ready for another Zoom meeting with her counselor. She had selected chamomile because of its calming properties. She also turned on a scented oil diffuser and had soft music in the background. Noel was intentionally creating an environment for her counseling sessions, one that would inspire a comforting and safe atmosphere.

"Looking at yourself through the lens of love, and not just any love but God's love, is more than sentiment, it is a critical step in recovering from self-loathing," the counselor told her in their third session.

Noel smiled; she had always thought of God's love as poetic and theological but not meaningfully personal.

Noel was excited to explore in greater depth what this meant.

The counselor shared her granddaughter's favorite Scripture verse: "*Do everything in love*—1 Corinthians 16:14. At seventeen years of age, my granddaughter has her finger on the pulse of God's most royal law. But my granddaughter would also be the first to admit that although she sees this verse as a standard of how she wants to treat others, she does not always apply it to how she treats herself. The truth is most of us don't."

"But what if we did?" the counselor asserted.

She continued. "Take, for instance, 1 Corinthians 13:4, which tells us, *love is patient, love is kind.* Imagine if we paraphrased the text with Noel speaking to Noel."

"Noel is patient, Noel is kind to Noel."

The counselor explained that the word *patient* means to "endure" or to "bear (suffer) long." *Kindness* is described as an "act of benevolence." "God's love patiently and kindly bears with our faulty self-perceptions while seeing all that we can be at the same time."

Noel thought about this for a moment. The counselor continued, "God wants us to have the same action of love (patience, kindness, and benevolence) toward ourselves."

Noel knew in her heart this was where she fell short—Noel was tough on herself.

The counselor pressed on. "We can find more insight by looking at the first phrase in the next verse of what love *does not* look like."

It does not envy. (v. 4)

Once again, Noel's counselor pulled out her Strong's dictionary to zero in on the word *envy*. "*Envy* is described as having 'a feeling of warmth *for* or *against*.'"

The counselor went on to share, "For some people, this unhealthy warmth drives them toward something. For you, Noel, it drove you away from something; it was a warmth *against*. In other words, something inwardly stirred you *against* yourself—to doubt yourself and not like yourself—which in effect ended your relationship with John."

This thought resonated with Noel. She'd struggled her whole life to be happy with who she was. She never felt like she measured up. She was envious of those who were in control of their expressions, and this caused unhealthy warmth against herself, and it had been this way for a long time. Noel was getting it; she had not been treating herself lovingly.

Noel was not patient or kind to—Noel.

Noel picked on—Noel.

Noel despised the personality of—Noel.

The counselor was able to help Noel trace this strong warmth of feeling against herself to her past, back to the neighborhood girls who had mistreated her. Noel was intent about not being seen as what she imagined in her own mind as a bubbly, naive person. She was envious of girls, and eventually women, who appeared cool and collected. In fact, this is how she saw Jan—as stylish, savvy, and confident.

The counselor was also able to show Noel that this same warmth against herself was manifesting in her present troubles. It didn't cause her to rise up and discredit Jan, but rather it discredited herself, taking her out of the equation altogether. Noel didn't want to be Noel, and in her mind, this meant being something different, stoic and in control.

"This is where you are experiencing the warmth of envy *toward* something," the counselor stated. "You want to be stoic. But in the pursuit of being stoic, you are missing out on the ways that God made you uniquely Noel—which incidentally was how John loved you." A look of sadness swept over Noel's face.

God had given Noel a beautiful and lively personality. Part of Noel's healing would be in seeing this aspect of herself in the light that God had made her this way. Up until this time, she had hated it and learned to manage it by stifling it (covering it up) because she internalized it as shame (or deficiency) and not the special quality that it was.

With the counselor's help, Noel was learning how to interrupt envy's compelling drive. When these feelings surfaced in the future, she would practice the new pattern of recognizing the intensity of the emotions as the inward alert system (flashing yellow sign) that she was about to enter self-loathing.

"Noel, it will take courage for you to explore the perception of yourself differently," the counselor said.

Noel understood this. She would need to trust God over the automatic negative self-talk that usually pervaded her mind whenever she had spurts of enthusiasm.

Noel prayed that she would have a better grasp of the ways God had fashioned who she was and the courage to openly value them, including her sunny disposition.

Incidentally, this also caused Noel to want to look at others differently—with the enduring patience and kind benevolence the counselor talked about from 1 Corinthians 13. *I want to kindly bear with others' faulty self-perceptions and see all that they can be at the same time*, Noel thought to herself.

For instance, when Steve had so adamantly relayed that John had *no* heart for Jan, this stirred in Noel a compassion for Jan, not that she was sorry John wasn't interested in Jan, but that perhaps Jan struggled to see herself as anything other than how she appeared.

She and Jan were of equal value, even though John preferred Noel. But John's heart for Noel wasn't based on one person being of greater significance (as we noted in Philippians 2:3 on being of equal value). It wasn't a winner or loser situation. Everyone is a work in progress. This truth of *mutuality* hit Noel.

Noel considered what God's enduring benevolent view of Jan might be, free from the need to impress people. Compassion replaced envy. When Noel went back to the campus, she was intentional about showing patience and kindness toward Jan.

Noel was coming to a fuller realization that if John truly was captivated by her personality, he was enjoying how God made her. She didn't have to fight so hard to be something different. Her counselor would tell her at the end of each session, "Remember, Noel, you don't want to settle for just 'accepting' yourself—you want to recognize that God made you unique and learn how to value who that is."

Although she'd lost John and was deeply saddened by this, she was on a discovery of who she is in the Lord, and this excited her.

2

John

John's heart lit up the first moment he ever laid eyes on Noel. Something about her was notably down-to-earth. On the first day of class, when the professor asked the students to share briefly what inspired them to take the course, John couldn't wait to hear from Noel.

"Hi, I'm Noel. I took this class for a better understanding of people, culture, and history." Noel's words were simple, clear, and understated.

How refreshing, John thought to himself. Everyone else had prattled on and on.

John couldn't help but notice the spark he saw in Noel's eyes, even with only the few words she spoke. He wanted to know more about her. But John soon found that a reserved demeanor was all Noel was willing to expose in class.

John wondered what Noel was like off campus.

Being a bit of a joker, John would insert sarcastic remarks during class lectures. Noel always smiled at his comic relief during the professor's orations. His timing was impeccable. It was never offensive, only light and humorous. This was part of John's disposition, and he knew it caused Noel to notice him.

After a certain amount of time had passed, John finally got up the nerve to ask Noel if she would like to review class notes for an upcoming exam at the local coffee shop. Students were encouraged to help each other this way. Noel was happy to have a study partner.

Their time together at the coffee shop was easy, and to the surprise of both, not awkward at all. John had a way of making everything comfortable. His personality was disarming and fun, and Noel's bursts of enthusiasm caused him great delight. John knew he had seen a spark in her eye from the very first day of class. But it never escaped his notice just how quickly Noel would slip back into reserved mode.

Soon their study adventures became wonderfully routine, exciting to be more precise. John had introduced Noel to a world of culinary adventure. Each time they met, John looked forward to the challenge of coaxing Noel out of her shell. Their friendship was natural and enjoyable. John often found himself lost in

Noel's big brown eyes and infectious laughter. Over the months they had grown close, having in-depth conversations about everything—the world, politics, faith, and many other shared interests.

Then one day out of the blue, when John came to class, there were no smiles from Noel in response to his usual levity. He tried some of his best material but to no avail.

Later that evening he called Noel, but she did not pick up the phone. He tried texting to engage in conversation, but she did not respond. John could feel that something was off. It was too silent. The next day, class was the same. Noel was aloof. He stepped in next to her as she was exiting the classroom. "Did you get my text about studying together?"

"Sorry, I've been busy, John. I'll check later," Noel said hastily as she dashed away.

Finally, after a few days a text showed up on John's phone from Noel. "I've decided to take the class more seriously and study on my own."

John was caught off guard by the dismissive nature of Noel's words. Initial feelings of anxiety caused him to continue to reach out, but he was met with detachment. Weeks went by with only silence.

Another young woman from class had been making great efforts to win John's attention since the start of the school year. Her name was Jan. Jan was stunning, and John had noticed, but he wasn't interested, not in the way she was at least. Nevertheless, Jan was confident and let her flirtatious moves toward John be known. It caused quite a stir on campus. Jan invited him to study outside of class, but John turned her down, not wanting to encourage a deeper connection.

Thinking it might be wiser, John invited a male friend from another class to study at the coffee shops he and Noel had frequented. Steve turned out to be a great study partner and ended up being an even greater listener and friend. Steve tuned in with sincere compassion when he learned of John's painful (and confusing) ghosting by a girl at the college.

Steve and John had several study sessions before Steve realized the girl who broke John's heart was his longtime neighbor and friend growing up—Noel. He was shocked and asked John if he could contact her for answers. "Please don't." John was insistent, and Steve honored this request but remained perplexed. He knew Noel, and she was a gem.

When John started dating one of Steve's fellow classmates named Holly, Steve decided to ask John again if he could talk to Noel. He suggested a conversation over Christmas break might provide clarity. John agreed but heavily cautioned Steve not to give Noel any hope—at all.

Steve was curious at John's strong stance, having seen the heartache John expressed over Noel, and not even that long ago.

Steve gently began to probe. "John, are you still in love with Noel?"

"Listen, I am not willing to entertain any ideas of Noel and I together."

Steve noticed that he didn't directly answer the question. Picking up once again on John's definitive tone, Steve decided to inquire about his past. "You know, John, I never asked you where you grew up," Steve said casually.

After about an hour of conversation, John had divulged quite a bit about his life. He told Steve he'd grown up in a small town and had parents who held high expectations. It became clear to Steve during this conversation that when those parental expectations were not fulfilled, John was met with long periods of silence. This caused John the anxiety of not knowing what he was doing wrong, along with feelings of failure.

Steve, being several years into his psychology studies, was able to assess that even though John loved Noel, Holly offered safety in an area John felt vulnerable. With Holly, John never worried about not knowing what was wrong or how to fix it. But this was because his heart did not run deep for Holly, which made it easy to be in a relationship with her. She was stable company, and that felt good.

PART 2

(John's emotions)

Steve mulled over his conversations with John in his mind. He knew replacing love with security might feel good to John temporarily, but in the long run the relationship would be missing an important component—being in love.

Steve also understood why this was happening in John's heart. When Noel went cold on John, he began experiencing fear and anxiety. It was the classic fight-or-flight response to Noel's aloofness. This caused John to move into his own form of self-preservation. He found himself in the arms of comfort, Holly.

John hadn't recognized that this was a pattern in his life.

As an adult, John no longer wanted to be beholden to the punishment of silence or the feelings of anxiety that followed him as a child. John's new girlfriend, Holly, was a natural encourager, and with her there would be no demands or high expectations.

The interesting thing was that Noel was not the

kind of person that held high expectations either. John had made a wrong assessment of Noel, based on Noel's wrong assessment of herself.

Noel, in response to her own inabilities and brokenness, simply shut down.

This translated as punishment to John. There were no answers, no efforts to grant understanding, no responsiveness—only silence, the kind John remembered enduring as a child—bouts of silence that resulted in feelings of shame for being a disappointment and not knowing why.

When Noel did not respond to John's texts, he wondered, *What have I done?*—the same question he asked himself over and over as child.

It was easy for Steve to see how these emotions transferred onto the predicament John found himself in with Noel.

John, like Noel, had trauma stored in the limbic system of his brain, and it automatically kicked in. It was self-talk that told him *failure was not worthy of explanation.* This would leave him to come up with his own ideas of how he was not measuring up—and he thought of plenty.

Steve decided to share a theory with John from one of his counseling classes. "There's something I learned you might find interesting."

John trusted Steve's words; he had proven to be a wise and good friend. So he listened.

Steve explained that studies reveal that childhood interactions with caregivers can shape a person's sense of self. "There are a few categories of 'attachment' we can fall into as children. Each represents a child's response to the kind of care they received."

Steve went on to present the different types:

There is *secure attachment*, when children are confident that their caregivers will be there for them when needed, even if temporarily separated.

Then there is *insecure avoidant attachment*, when children are independent, anxious, and avoid seeking comfort from their caregiver.

There is also *insecure resistant attachment*, when children are clingy and overly anxious when separated from their caregiver and not comforted upon their return.

Finally, there is *disorganized attachment*, with unpredictable behavior and difficulty regulating emotions.

John recognized right away which category he fell into—the insecure avoidant attachment. When he was young, he did not feel secure in his parents' care, especially during silent treatments.

"A child has no other frame of reference in their early years, so what they experience becomes normalized to them," Steve shared. "That is, until it no longer is."

"What do you mean?" John asked.

Steve went on to explain, "You did not realize that life could be different until later, when you began to experience life outside the home environment. But even though you were thriving out in the world, you were and still are vulnerable as it relates to emotions of attachment."

John was quietly listening as Steve continued, "Silence, no matter what the reason, provokes anxiety for you. Even if it's silence for reasons besides failure to meet expectations. Silence for you is a trauma association."

Unfortunately, Noel had no idea she had stepped on this hornet's nest of vulnerability when ghosting John.

How could she know? She had her own issues to work through. And for that matter, how could John know about Noel? He had issues too.

Nevertheless, John was thankful that by God's grace, the painful loss of their relationship had brought him into a solid friendship with Steve.

John was beginning to recognize that there was a correlation between his upbringing and self-loathing. Up until now, anxiety and then turning to safety was an automatic mode for him when encountering silence or aloofness. Even with John's great personality, popularity, humor, stability, and all-around good character, he still struggled when it came to attachment.

⁂

Steve pondered the psychological angles of his conversations with John. Steve knew that all people have masks or modes of safety to help them deal with pain or heartache in life; typically, things they already have a propensity toward. For instance: charm, beauty, style, intelligence, talent, competition, sports, money, hospitality, service, humor, etc. These often become the areas people plunge into to offset feelings of self-loathing.

Steve recognized that John's comedic personality masked his heartache growing up. John's humor had helped him greatly.

It was a kind of crutch. But Steve also understood from his studies that crutches provide needed support. As long as the person using them eventually discovers that they are valuable beyond their masks.

Steve had his own mask of dealing with difficulty. Being a listening ear came naturally to Steve. He was good at helping others. But it was harder for Steve to accept help, and he knew it. This was part of the reason he was pursuing psychology. Sure, he wanted to help people like John, but he also wanted to understand his own mind better. In fact, one of Steve's favorite quotes about understanding psychology comes from researcher Beatrice Beebe, who said, "Most research is me-search."

PART 3

(The lens of faith-direction)

John was inspired by Steve's unusual faith. It didn't surprise him though; Steve had mentioned that he considered becoming a pastor before entering the study of psychology. Steve believed that pastoring and counseling were similar. He would often say that shepherding souls (and mental health) went hand in hand.

John trusted Steve and asked if he would consider helping him work through his propensity toward self-loathing. Steve had grown to appreciate John like a brother. "This will be good practice for future counseling too," Steve told him.

But Steve, like Noel's counselor, was certain that true healing would depend on how John sees God—and how John believes God sees him. So this is where he started.

Going back to the subject of caregivers, Steve explained that people often view God with a similar lens to their guardians when they are young. Based on previous conversations, Steve had a suspicion this might be the case for John.

Steve shared his own miscalculated view of God from his childhood. "It wasn't from my caregivers, per se, but from convoluted ideas forged together while in their care," he told John.

Here's what happened.

While driving with my family as a young boy up a steep, winding, mountainous road, I sensed the frustration brewing in the car. So I asked my family, "Who lives up here?"

And because the mountain was so high up in the sky, my grandmother sarcastically replied, "God, that's who!"

With those words said, I was eager to get to the top for a glimpse of where God lives. Finally making it to the pinnacle, we spotted a water tower set on top of gravel. As my family stepped out of the car to stretch their legs, an old man with a white beard emerged from a small shack.

In a scolding tone he hollered, "No trespassing here!"

All of us scurried back into the car quickly and made our long journey back down the mountain.

But from that point on, and for many years, in my mind I had met God—and He wasn't very nice!

No one had bothered to explain that this wasn't really where God lived—and I never asked.

Finishing his story, Steve said, "As a boy, I would tell people I saw God—He's got a white beard and is mean!"

John couldn't help but laugh.

Steve added, "That impression took some work to undo."

"What impressions do you have when you think of God?" Steve asked.

John thought about it for a moment. "I guess I have always thought of Him as having high expectations."

"I had a feeling this might be the case," Steve replied. After further conversation Steve was able to assess that John's parents had passed their performance expectations into John's formative thoughts of God.

Luke 2 came to Steve's mind. "Have you ever read about how Jesus at age twelve went missing from his parents for three days?"

"Yes, I always wondered about that," John said.

Steve continued. "They were so upset and frantic trying to find Him. They finally found Jesus in the temple surrounded by the teachers, who were amazed by Him."

A bit perplexed, John asked, "What about Jesus letting His parents down?"

"You're right, they felt let down. Verse 48 tells us

that his mother asked Jesus why He had treated them like this."

"Oh, I can't wait to hear your psychological interpretation," John responded.

"Well, it's not so much about psychology as it is direction," Steve remarked. "God had already revealed the direction of Jesus's life to Mary and Joseph in dreams years prior, and it was different from what they (as His parents) expected in this moment. Jesus asked His parents this question—'Didn't you know I had to be in my Father's house?' "

"That's interesting," John replied.

Steve continued. "Here's another story of Mary's expectation not being met by Jesus. In Mark 3, when a crowd had gathered around Jesus, someone told Him that His mother and brothers were outside looking for Him. Jesus, looking at the circle of people near Him, replied, 'Here are my mother and my brothers.' "

"Wow, that must have felt dismissive to His mother!" John said.

The point Steve was trying to make was that in Mary's humanity, she had expectations for her son that, at times, were different from God's direction for Jesus.

Steve explained that John's parents' expectations had become so intertwined with what they taught him about God as a child that it shaped a faulty sense in his heart that God held the same expectations.

Steve went on to share that getting to know God as

different from a performance taskmaster would benefit not only his soul but his mind too.

"Humble, gentle Jesus's direction is merciful and filled with grace—much different from your parents' expectations," Steve said.

Steve wanted John to be free to discover Jesus in a new way, no longer holding his parents' interpretations as the standard. The silence his parents often exhibited, making him feel like a failure, was not how God saw John. Learning to separate these two realities would take time but would be tremendously healing.

Steve also shared that one of the ways John had handled these difficult feelings over the years was to hide behind a mask.

"This was a way of protecting your heart," Steve said.

As Steve said these things, Holly immediately came to John's mind. He recognized that as much he liked and appreciated Holly, he wasn't in love with her, and it wasn't fair to hide behind her in this way. He knew breaking up with her meant he would be alone and vulnerable, but this would be a season to grow.

Steve and John began doing a weekly Bible study together. And it was nothing like he had experienced as a child with rigid rules, guilt, or expectations. It was not his parents' way of religion but a new direction of faith, based on getting to know a loving Savior who valued him, mistakes and all.

3

Holly

olly used cosmetics to try to conceal her red nose and puffy eyes from a full night of crying. She didn't want to go to class but knew playing catch-up from missing a few days would make life even harder. Holly was hurting. She was still trying to grasp why her relationship with John had to end—they were good together. She was sure of it. John had told her many times about how good he felt being with her.

Holly arrived while class was already in session. As soon as she got settled in her seat, she looked up and saw John's friend Steve a few rows ahead. He was listening studiously as the professor lectured. Holly became distracted. *I wonder if Steve knows that John broke up with me.* Holly and Steve had become friends through John.

They were in several classes together, both on a similar academic track—psychology.

"What's your hypothesis on this, Holly?" the professor asked with a projected voice. Caught off guard by all eyes looking her direction, Holly simply said, "I'm not sure. I need a bit more information." This answer appeased the teacher. He liked it when the students thought deeper about concepts and ideas.

Steve couldn't help but notice Holly's eyes were red. His heart sank. He knew John was planning to break up with her; he just didn't know when. He said a silent prayer. *God, please comfort Holly.*

After class Holly made a beeline toward Steve. "Hi Steve, I guess you heard about John and me." Her eyes searching his, Steve looked at her with deep compassion. "I'm sorry, Holly."

"I would like to understand it better, though, Steve," Holly said.

Steve could see Holly was looking for closure, "I can ask John if he would be willing to connect," he said gently.

"I don't think he would tell me anything new. Maybe you could ask him if he would mind if I got a fresh perspective from a trusted friend, like you."

Steve felt the weight of this responsibility. "Let me see what I can do," he said, leaning in to give Holly an affirming side hug.

"Thanks," she said with a quivering smile.

Holly went home from campus that day reeling inside. But she couldn't quite put her finger on why. Her heart was saddened over the breakup, this was true, but she also realized that she and John had not been dating that long. She had survived breakups before. Why did this one seem different? Unfortunately, self-loathing thoughts came rushing to her mind: *I failed. I wasn't enough. What kind of counselor doesn't know how to be a good girlfriend?*

The next day at school, Holly saw Steve walking up the campus steps. It was earlier than usual for them both to be at the university. Holly had barely slept the previous night and couldn't stand being at home any longer. It caused her to overthink. At least her studies would give her a break from the onslaught of negative self-talk. She could go and review notes for an upcoming quiz. Meanwhile, Steve was there early hoping to run into Holly.

"Steve!" A voice rang out from a distance.

Steve turned around to see Holly walking toward him. *Great timing, Lord, thank you,* he said in another silent prayer. As Holly made her way up the steps, Steve went over his recent conversation with John in his mind. He wanted to honor John's privacy and represent him well. John had given Steve his trust to talk to Holly.

"Do you have time to grab a cup of coffee at the campus cafe" Steve asked.

"Yes, thanks Steve. That sounds good."

They settled at a table off to the side with their drinks. Holly had selected a caramel macchiato and Steve a double espresso. Steam was rising off their hot beverages, "That'll get your day going," Holly said, smiling.

"Early mornings require a bit of a jump start for me," Steve responded with a grin. He continued, "I talked with John, and he was happy if I could help with any confusion you might feel."

"That's just the thing," Holly said, "I was tossing and turning all night trying to figure out why I am so bothered since we hadn't been dating that long." Steve listened quietly as Holly shared her thoughts.

"Part of it was the shock of the breakup, since it seemed to be going so well."

"Can you share what those markers were that made you feel like all was going well?"

"For one thing, he seemed very responsive, and his countenance would lift whenever I was around," Holly replied. "I could tell he struggled with being down quite a bit; I think it was expectations his parents had on him."

"That is very perceptive, Holly," Steve added.

Holly looked at Steve and smiled. It lightened her heart to be thought of in a positive way during this difficult time. *Why can't I do this for myself*, she wondered.

A loud bell rang, signaling classes were about to start. Their time was up just as they were getting into the conversation. Steve suggested meeting after school at a local diner he often visited. "It has the best fries in town," he said casually. Holly liked the idea. She barely had eaten the day before. A large basket of fries sounded comforting.

⚹

When Holly walked into the diner, Steve was already sitting in a booth. He motioned for her to join him. Holly flung her book bag into the inside of the bench and slid in. "It smells dinery in here," she said, taking in a deep breath.

"Dinery—I've never heard that term. I like it," Steve said with a warm smile.

Holly grabbed the menu and began surveying the options. "What's good here?"

"The double-decker bacon and cheddar burger," Steve said without hesitation.

"I think I'll try that," Holly replied enthusiastically. Although Holly was a grilled cheese fan, she always loved the idea of trying something new. Steve marveled at the thought of this petite human eating a double cheeseburger.

"John has a more refined palate, and that generally means smaller portions," Holly explained. "I'm hungry and I'm going for it."

Steve and Holly talked for hours—interestingly, very little about John. It was surprising how much Steve and Holly had in common. But when the subject of John did come up, it became apparent to Steve why Holly might be struggling with closure. Holly was a natural encourager; one might even say she was a fixer. When Holly and John connected, it was in a distressing season for John. Holly could see that her words of encouragement were a comfort.

Steve surmised that Holly got so lost in the "fixing" part of her relationship with John that his abrupt departure left her feeling inadequate in the career path she had chosen. When it got right down to it, the breakup made Holly feel like a failure.

Steve posed this possibility gently, expressing that although John did feel safe with Holly, it was not enough to build a romantic relationship. Holly's eyes grew wide as she took in his words. It was a moment of clarity—a recognition. The propensity toward self-loathing was more about Holly's internal performance evaluation and less about deep feelings for John.

PART 2

(Holly's emotions)

Holly had never considered that her natural gift of encouragement could also have a negative side. Her friend Steve had used the word *fixer*.

Admittedly, Holly loved the idea of helping people. But the idea of *needing* to fix others struck her. She had progressed far enough in psychology to interpret this to be more about her, rather than those she was trying to help. This became clear as she conversed with Steve about her breakup with John.

The truth was that Holly was incredibly talented. All her life she was told that she was gifted when it came to wisdom and common sense. She was the person everyone gravitated toward whenever there was a conflict. When the time came to go to university, she already knew what her major would be; all her friends did too—psychology!

She had become accustomed to success in this area. Of course, not in every case, but it had never hit her this hard. This time it seemed different. *Perhaps the pain of this breakup was providential,* she thought to herself, *a learning experience.* This was how she wanted to view it, anyway. Holly was humbled.

Steve had asked Holly if she wanted to talk through it further, which she did. "Let's meet back here at the diner on Saturday at noon, if it works for your schedule," he said.

"I'll be here, but next time I'll be ordering the deluxe grilled cheese," Holly replied with a smile.

It was two days until Saturday, which gave Holly plenty of time for introspection. She thought about John and how she had read him well. She had correctly suggested to Steve that she thought John struggled with his parents' high expectations. *Did I use that insight to manipulate a relationship with John?* Holly wondered. *Did I do it to feel good about myself?* It came so naturally she hadn't even realized it. When the relationship failed, she felt like she failed, as if she had no value because her value was in the success of her gift.

Her conversation with Steve played over again in her head. "We all have the propensity for our self-esteem to crumble if our talents don't measure up to our expectations," Steve had shared. "The problem is that sometimes we think *we are* our talents and abilities. Society even promotes this idea. It's easy to get caught up in having our identities so entwined with our gifted areas."

Steve had explained how this applies to privilege too. Those who are at an advantage are often successful and feel mistakenly entitled. "This can even happen to ministry leaders. Celebrity treatment, larger offices, and various perks become expected. And if for some reason these abilities, gifts, or privileges stop, the people with these advantages are not sure who they are or what their purpose is." Steve shared with Holly that one of his closest friends, a very popular pastor, became very unpopular after an upset in the church. "His sense of identity fell apart," Steve continued. "Remarkably, this is when he learned his true value in Christ."

❧

On Saturday Holly was eager to meet with Steve and arrived at the diner a few minutes early. She spotted the booth where they ate two days earlier; it was available. She slid in the side facing the door this time. The bells hanging from the entrance handle jingled every time the door opened. Holly loved that sound. Each time she heard it, she looked in anticipation. The next jingle was Steve walking through the door.

"Good morning, or should I say good afternoon?" Holly exclaimed as Steve approached the booth.

"Well, looking at my watch, it's 11:58, so it could be either," Steve said with a grin. Steve had a way of making people feel comfortable. He scooted into the booth opposite Holly.

Holly wasted no time and started talking. "I was thinking about our conversations, Steve, and some thoughts came up I wanted to share." Steve gave an encouraging nod.

"I noticed that after John broke up with me, I was not myself. It was as if I lost all good sense." Steve listened as Holly continued. "Somehow, I became a different person. For instance, when John said he was going through some difficulties and thought we should just be friends, I found myself acting desperate, even saying things to subvert his decision." Steve gave a reassuring smile, acknowledging Holly's words.

"I was confused," Holly continued. "My friend told me she hadn't seen John as happy as when he was with me." Steve quietly took this all in. Holly was impressed at Steve's listening skills. He made her feel valuable and not judged.

"I'm curious. Was your friend surprised when John broke up with you?" Steve asked.

Holly paused for a moment before she spoke. "To be honest, my friend is the one who introduced me to John. She originally had a heart for John, but John did not reciprocate those feelings."

Holly didn't answer the question directly, and Steve wondered who this person was. *It couldn't be Noel because their feelings were mutual*, he thought to himself.

"My friend was sure John and I were perfect for each other. She knew his former crush and was convinced John and I would be compatible," Holly shared.

At this point Steve was almost certain Holly was

talking about Jan. But not wanting to become biased, Steve decided not to ask. He just continued to listen.

"I hesitated at first because of her heart for him, but she insisted that she would get over it." Holly relayed this to Steve almost in a questioning tone.

"You weren't sure you believed her?" Steve inquired.

"It just seemed odd, but at the same time generous," Holly added.

Holly and Steve talked for hours. Steve suggested that the behavior Holly noticed about herself—acting like a different person—might be stemming from the *fixer* in her. "It comes with a feeling of losing control in an area you feel confident in," he said.

Loss of confidence is a huge catalyst in self-loathing. Self-loathing beats it down even further; Holly could see that clearly. Steve went on to share that John's rejection wasn't a rejection of Holly as a person, even though she had received it that way. Holly had even questioned whether she was in the right field. The truth was that John did feel better when he was around Holly. But he did not want to use her that way any longer. John knew Holly deserved to be truly loved, and Steve knew it too.

Steve suggested to Holly that separating out who she is from the gifts God had given her would help her navigate future relationships. Holly was grateful for these conversations with Steve. Not only did she find clarification, but she also felt a new sense of direction. The next big question on Holly's mind was how to go about this.

Leaving an extra-large tip on the table for taking the booth for so long, Holly and Steve headed out the diner door as the bells on the handle jingled.

PART 3

(The lens of spiritual pursuit)

Steve's words replayed in Holly's mind—*separating out who you are from the gifts God has given you will help you navigate future relationships.*

As interested as Holly was in navigating relationships better, she also wanted to do this for herself, not just relationships.

She also thought about how Steve said it is not simply a psychological pursuit, but more importantly a spiritual one. After a week of contemplation and still feeling confused, she decided to ask Steve personally after class.

Steve knew this would take more than a quick hallway conversation, so he suggested meeting again at the diner the following Saturday. "Thanks, Steve," Holly said with a relieved smile. He gave her a comforting side hug and a wink. His unexpected wink caused Holly's heart to flutter. She dismissed it quickly; feelings for

Steve were the last thing she needed right now.

As Saturday came closer, Steve sent Holly a text. "How does breakfast sound instead of lunch? The diner has a great breakfast menu." Holly was all about breakfast; it was her favorite meal. She happily agreed. Meanwhile, she began putting together a list of questions to bring to her meeting with Steve. Holly was organized this way.

The breakfast crowd was different. Even the smell was distinct. Scents of bacon, scrambled eggs, and cinnamon buns wafted through the air. "Fresh coffee?" the waitress inquired. "Please!" Holly said without hesitation. Steve smiled. Based on Holly's previous lunch selections, he couldn't help but wonder what impressive order she would be making for breakfast. "I think I'll have the farm fresh egg sausage scramble," Holly said to the waitress.

Is that it? Steve wondered.

Holly continued, "Also, can I have hash browns and grits on the side? And an everything bagel toasted with butter?"

There it is, Steve thought to himself with delight.

Holly and Steve enjoyed their meal and talked about many things before Holly pulled out her notepad with a list.

"What is this?" Steve inquired.

"It's my list of questions," Holly said with a grin.

"You're serious business, Holly Madison."

Steve motioned for the waitress to bring more coffee. Holly blushed and proceeded to talk. "Here's number one—what exactly do you mean by separating out who I am from the gifts God has given me?"

Steve paused for a moment and said, "Before answering, I want to emphasize how important it is to see the spiritual position and pursuit."

Holly said, "That was number two on my list."

"Let's switch these around," Steve said.

"Okay."

Steve continued, "The truth is, it is the same question, but the order within the question is what makes a difference."

"How so?" Holly asked.

"Prioritizing our spiritual position to and pursuit of God with our gifts and talents places them in God's hands." Holly was listening intently. Steve went on. "The opposite is centering our attention on our gifts and talents, which focuses on the gift rather than the gift giver. This explains our often self-driven uses of them." Holly was quietly taking this in. "If we don't prioritize the spiritual," Steve said, "we can become so intertwined with our gifts that we have a hard time seeing ourselves outside of them. Then when they don't perform as hoped, our hearts become crushed."

"Gosh," Holly said, shaking her head.

Steve wasn't sure if Holly's response was one of being encouraged or discouraged. He went on. "But if our spiritual connection to God is the priority instead, it allows us to become intertwined with God in a way that when we exercise our gifts and talents, we see them separately from who we are. In essence our gifts become an extension or conduit that God can use, so even when things don't go well or as expected, we are okay."

Holly's mind was whirling, but it wasn't a bad thing. She remembered what Steve had said about his popular pastor friend in their previous meeting. There was a great discovery waiting for his friend in his "failure to succeed as usual." It redirected his focus and dependence on God. But it also helped him see that failure in his talents didn't make him less valuable. Instead of self-deprecating and agonizing over her perceived failure with John, perhaps for Holly, like Steve's friend, it was an opportunity for discovery.

After a moment of silence Holly said, "You know, Steve, psychology isn't all about helping others; it's also an opportunity to learn how to think well for ourselves."

"I couldn't agree more!" Steve replied. He continued the thought. "In fact, I sincerely believe that faith and psychology go hand in hand. God cares about our mental health as well as our soul health."

"I have one more verse I'd like to share, Holly, before they kick us out." They had already overstayed a reasonable time limit at the diner—again. Thankfully, Steve was familiar with the staff there and they liked him. They thought of him as part of the diner family.

"First Corinthians 4:7 talks about our gifts." Steve pulled out his phone and googled the verse so he could read it to Holly.

For who makes you different from anyone else? What do you have that you did not receive? And if you did receive it, why do you boast as though you did not?

"I never thought about our personal abilities this way, Steve," Holly said.

Steve paused but then added softly, "But often, we pursue them as if God is *not* the benefactor."

Holly looked saddened. "I can see now that I used my gift of encouragement not only to try to fix John but also so I could feel good about myself."

Steve looked compassionately into Holly's eyes "We are all self-driven unless we pursue the spiritual. It's an ongoing, moment by moment reorientation." Holly's eyes filled with tears.

Steve was moved by Holly's vulnerability. "I have a confession of my own to make," he said. Holly looked at him with curiosity. "John told me your favorite meal is breakfast. That's why I invited you to meet me in the morning. I was trying to impress you." A gentle smile swept over Holly's face.

4

Steve

Steve knew he needed to tell John that he'd developed a crush on Holly. He just didn't know quite how yet. John had trusted Steve to talk with Holly on his behalf after the breakup, but now he was falling for her. He wasn't sure if Holly had feelings for him or not, but it didn't matter. Steve felt a mixture of guilt and shame, but most of all he felt undeserving. This was not unusual for Steve, though. It had been a nagging feeling that went as far back as he could remember. "Good things" were meant for others.

Negative thoughts began to fill Steve's mind. *How could I have done this to John?, How could I have added more stress to Holly?, What kind of a friend am I to either of them?* Of course, these thoughts made him feel undeserving of either.

Steve decided to put off his Bible study with John to get his head in a better space; they were supposed to meet in an hour. This was a good time to go on a prayer walk as he often did. He'd been so distracted that prayer was not coming easily. Steve grabbed a water bottle and headed out the door. Living only a few blocks from a nature walking path, he enjoyed looking at the beauty of creation. The Scripture about how God takes care of the wildflowers came to his mind; this was a soothing thought. Steve related to the wildflowers in a way. He had always felt like a wanderer, never really belonging anywhere and randomly being everywhere. He connected with nature. The quiet and calm was just what he needed.

Steve was almost back home from his walk when a text sounded on his phone. "Hi Steve, this is Holly, I was wondering if we could meet at the diner on Saturday?" Steve did not immediately respond. Conflicting emotions came over him as he read her text. On the one hand, he really wanted to see Holly, but on the other he felt a great loyalty to John and knew he needed to talk with him first. He also remembered the trigger of silence John felt when Noel was unresponsive, and he didn't want Holly to feel that from him. So he prayed, right there on his way home. *God, please give me wisdom.*

Steve remembered a paper he had written, "Managing Emotions from a Faith-Based Perspective." The subject was intentional pausing. More specifically, it described the practice of deliberately delaying a pressing urge to react.

Steve knew that based on how he was feeling, this was the right time to exercise this kind of pausing. When he got home, he began thumbing through his files looking for his notes. *Here they are*, he said to himself with a sigh of relief. As he read, he paused between each entry slowly and deliberately, taking in one thought at a time:

Note: Intentional pausing helps separate an emotion I am experiencing from who I am as a person.

Steve paused and silently responded to this thought in his mind. *Even though I'm feeling shame, I am not the shame.*

Note: I am not defined by other people's emotions about me.

Steve paused and remembered how important this principle was. *I am afraid of John's negative feelings toward me, but even if he thinks poorly of me, I will be okay.*

Note: Intentional pausing acts as a cognitive switch, allowing me to access another part of my brain that God designed to help me understand and reason. This is the logic section of the brain, the frontal lobe (the reasoning center). Here I can contemplate my emotions as data.

This is what I really need right now—to reason this through. Finally,

> Note: Emotions are loaded with information we can sort through to understand better why we respond the way we do. God not only advocates for this kind of reasoning but He also invites it: "*Come now, let us reason together, says the Lord*" (Isaiah 1:18 ESV).

This amazes me—I can explore my emotions with God's help from the reasoning section of my brain, Steve thought to himself. He felt comforted.

Applying this intentional pause helped Steve self-regulate. He started feeling more grounded and able to pursue the conversations that he knew awaited with both John and Holly. The exercise also made Steve eager to discover what some of his emotions meant and why he was experiencing them.

Again, this was one of the reasons Steve was pursuing the field of psychology—to understand himself better. He thought about his favorite quote: *Research is me-search.*

Steve was ready to contact his two friends. First, he texted John and asked if he was free one afternoon during the week to meet at the bistro where they often studied. Then Steve texted Holly to let her know he could meet her on Saturday at the diner.

John was curious as to why Steve had requested a meeting. When Steve sat down at the bistro table, John asked, "Is everything okay, buddy?" Steve calmly but apologetically shared that he had developed a heart for Holly.

"What, is that all?" John replied. "This is great news!" Steve was caught off guard by John's gracious response. John continued, "I always thought you two made a better match."

Steve marveled as he took in John's words.

As Steve processed, he recognized that his feelings and emotions of shame and guilt were different from how John reacted (no guilt or shame). It reminded him of the truth in the intentional pause exercise. Emotions are separate from who we are as a person—and sometimes far from what's really going on. Steve was glad he did not allow his emotions or his fear of John's reaction to take over.

"How does Holly feel about you?" John asked.

"I don't know," Steve replied. "She asked to meet this Saturday, and I'm not sure how it will go."

Steve knew it would be a good idea to practice the pausing exercise again before meeting up with Holly.

PART 2

(Steve's emotions)

"I'm glad you suggested breakfast instead of lunch, Steve," Holly said with a playful smile.

Steve wondered what Holly thought of him. *What a jerk she must think I am*, he said to himself as he reminisced about flirting with her the last time they were together at breakfast. As soon as he had this thought, he recognized his emotions were trying to take the lead. Immediately Steve reflected on the pausing exercise he'd done before coming to the diner. He quickly counteracted the negative thought with a new thought—*I am not going to let my emotions take over*. So he didn't.

"I know how you love breakfast," Steve said with a wink. He couldn't help himself.

Holly melted. She'd forgotten how Steve's charming winks made her feel like there were butterflies in her belly. She liked that feeling.

Holly spoke up. "Steve, the reason I wanted to meet was to thank you for your help in working through closure with John." Steve gave Holly an acknowledging smile. "You know," she continued, "I don't really know very much about you."

"What do you want to know?" Steve asked casually. Holly paused and thought for a moment.

The waitress arrived with steaming plates of food. After setting everything out on the table, she remarked, "Stay as long as you two lovebirds need; good conversation and good food take time."

Holly chuckled. Steve gently corrected the waitress. "We're not a couple, just good friends from class." The waitress apologized, but her face was not convinced as she walked away. She remembered them taking the booth for hours before.

"Well, I guess since we are 'good friends,' I really should know a little more about you," Holly mused.

Steve smiled. "Okay, what's your question?"

"I hope this is not too personal," Holly began, "but why are you still single?"

Steve leaned back, and after a short hesitation he answered, "I guess I haven't found the right girl."

"Hmm," Holly said while searching his eyes.

Steve was calmly guarded, and he knew it. But he also knew Holly was a psych major and would not settle for such a general response.

"Do you mind if I ask you if you have ever had a serious relationship?" Holly inquired.

Steve could tell Holly wanted to know more, so he entertained her question. "I have had several relationships but nothing serious."

"So, you've never had your heart broken?"

"I wouldn't say that."

"Interesting," Holly said inquisitively. She was processing Steve's answers in her mind.

After taking several bites in silence, Holly probed further. "No serious relationships, yet your heart has been broken. It sounds like maybe you had a heart for someone other than the women in the relationships you describe as, quote unquote, 'nothing serious.' "

Steve was impressed with Holly's clinical-like deductions. "You might say that."

Resting her elbows on the table and chin on her hands, Holly responded, "Now I'm intrigued."

The truth was that Steve had a heart for a few girls in his past, but there were always one or two of his guy friends also interested. So he did not pursue them. In a sense, Steve's heartbreaks were always silent in nature.

"Wait a minute," Holly asserted. "This means that those 'nothing serious' relationships you were in were safe, like John and me?"

Steve looked like his mind was clicking. "Maybe that's why I could relate," he replied.

Steve had always seen himself as the wingman and not the leading man, and he was a good one. He could be the best of friends with anyone, like he was with Noel and John. But the deeper he felt about a girl, the more he thought she deserved someone better.

Growing up, Steve did not have a very good sense of self. He had always felt lost in the crowd of his family. Everyone took precedence because they went after it; the result was that Steve was often overlooked. This is common in busy families. He picked things up on his own along the way, like figuring out the mean man with a white beard on top of a mountain was not really God. No one had bothered to tell him. He was a wanderer of sorts, always finding random community, like with the people in the diner. He was a regular there, and he felt connected.

"Okay," said Holly. "What about the girls you did have a heart for—what held you back?"

"I'm not an aggressive person," Steve stated. "If a friend of mine felt like they were a better fit with a girl I cared for, I was happy to let them explore the possibility."

Holly looked at Steve intently, trying to make sense of his reasoning. She knew that he was true-blue at heart, not a game player. She liked that about him. But she also surmised that he held himself back.

Steve was good at self-control. Maybe too good. Steve had an unusual grasp on the verse Proverbs 16:32, "*Better a patient person than a warrior, one with self-control than one who takes a city.*" At the young age of ten, Steve had been introduced to this Scripture by a neighborly grandmother who lived next door.

Steve was sitting under a tree (in her front yard), tearfully fuming after a scuffle with some kids who lived on that street, when the older woman noticed him from her kitchen window. She made her way outside with a tall glass of lemonade and a small sack over her shoulder. Gently sitting down next to him she said, "I just made this fresh, Steve; I thought it might make you feel better." And it did! "You know, when I was young, I held a verse in my heart that helped me when I felt mad, sad, or overwhelmed."

She proceeded to share with Steve that he, too, could be greater than a warrior if he prayed and asked God for self-control. "This could be your superpower, just like a superhero," Miss Vera shared. Then Miss Vera opened her bag and pulled out a plaque with the verse on it. She had taken it off her own wall when she noticed Steve's frustration outside. Someone had given it to her when she was young too. Steve put that verse in his room. He treasured it and looked at it regularly.

It was no surprise that Steve would grow up and write a brilliant and meaningful paper on intentional pausing and the power of applying self-control. Miss Vera had long since passed, but her small gift had big implications, helping him throughout the years.

Sitting at the diner with Holly, Steve became lost in thought, reflecting on Miss Vera's kindness toward him.

"What are you thinking about, Steve?" Holly asked with interest.

Steve shared with Holly about Miss Vera and the verse's impact on his life. Holly took it in, pondering his every word as they lingered over hot coffee. *No wonder Steve has such good self-control,* she thought to herself.

"Steve?"

"Yes?"

"Have you ever caught yourself breaking that cool exterior of self-control toward any of those girls you cared for? You know, like flirting with them?" Holly's eye contact changed from playful to serious.

"Only once," Steve said.

Holly knew in her heart Steve was talking about her and his impromptu confession of knowing she liked breakfast.

Their eyes locked and the diner became still, as if no one else was in the room, even though it was busy and loud. Hours passed. The waitress walked up with a big smile and asked, "More coffee for my two *good friends*?" It was obvious that hearts were connecting, even to Holly and Steve.

PART 3

(The lens of truth)

Both Steve and Holly were floating on a cloud. Weeks had gone by, and love was in the air. They couldn't believe how much they had in common; even their career pursuits were on the same track. But there was still hesitation from Steve, and Holly could feel it. On a particular Friday night while out on a date, they ran into a mutual professor. "Well!" said Professor Stan with an endearing smile, "I had no idea you two were dating."

Stiffening a bit, Steve replied, "We're just spending some time together outside of class."

Holly surveyed Steve's countenance to try to make sense of his odd statement. She remembered him saying something similar to the waitress right before they started dating.

Holly had noticed on more than one occasion that Steve had acted detached from the relationship. But this time it caused her to toss and turn at night. She knew he loved her, and she felt secure in this but couldn't quite pinpoint the reason for the discrepancy in his behavior.

Holly decided to send Steve an early morning text: "Can we meet for breakfast at the diner?"

When Steve walked through the diner door, the jingling bells broke and crashed to the floor. Holly wasn't the superstitious type, but somehow it unsettled her heart. The waitress scooped up the bells and tossed them in a nearby drawer. Steve walked over and slid in the booth. "Is everything all right?"

"Steve," Holly began, "the real question is, is everything okay with us?"

Steve was not expecting this response. As far as he knew everything was great, better than great. "I think we are doing amazing, Holly. What makes you ask that question?"

"When Professor Stan mentioned not realizing that we were dating, you seemed to downplay it." Holly was direct.

Steve lowered his eyes a bit in thought. "You're right," he said. It came so automatically he hadn't even noticed. "You can be certain, Holly, it was not from any lack of love."

Holly knew this, but it felt reassuring to hear those words. "I have experienced this on several occasions from you, Steve."

Steve wanted to know what those occasions were, not only to rectify them in Holly's mind but also to try to piece together what was behind them.

They placed a breakfast order, knowing this would take time.

Talking back and forth through the details while eating French toast slathered with cinnamon butter and syrup was cathartic. Holly asked, "Do you remember the feelings that surfaced when Dr. Stan made a comment about us dating?"

Steve quietly reflected. Several seconds went by. Finally, Steve spoke. "I felt undeserving to be with such an amazing woman." Holly's eyes lit up as if multiple light bulbs were going off in her head at once.

"Steve, from what you have shared with me about your life, you have always felt undeserving. Part of the way you have managed this in the past was to exercise self-control over your emotions. You were blessed by your neighbor, Miss Vera who guided you this way. I'm sure this was God's protection and provision for you. And you have helped so many others because of this beautiful fruit of the Spirit, self-control, even writing a paper about intentional pausing."

Steve was listening intently as Holly continued.

"But now, it might be time to embrace and welcome some emotions that are vulnerable."

"I think I have with you, Holly; my emotions come easy with you," Steve responded.

"Yes," Holly said, "but they are not coming easy with others. You feel safe with me, Steve, but bottled up with others, undeserving. Almost apologetic."

Steve was struck by this. He marveled at Holly's insight.

Steve had always felt *less-than* because he had less than most. He had perceived at an early age that the world values those with more. Because of this Steve felt safest in the support role and not the lead. The gift he had been given by Miss Vera, the verse on self-control, had helped him become strong, just like she had said—it became his superpower. It served him well, and others through him. In essence, for many years he played the leading role of a wingman in everyone else's life.

Steve was being challenged by Holly to see value differently when it came to himself. Holly reminded Steve that God esteems those who are poor in spirit and circumstances. Holly knew that Steve was "poor" in self-value. She wrote a verse on a napkin and slid it across the table to Steve.

It was James 2:5, which says, *"Has not God chosen those who are poor in the eyes of the world to be rich in faith?"* Steve had always lacked privilege, but when it came to faith, he was very rich. Steve picked up the napkin and read the words as a smile came across his face.

"It's my turn, Steve, to be there for you," Holly said lovingly. "I'm sure you are familiar with what the word *truth* means in Ephesians 6—when it talks about standing firm with the belt of truth buckled around your waist?"

"Yes, it means 'not false,' " Steve said, wondering where Holly was headed with this thought.

"And to that point—the Greek word for truth,

altheia, means, 'the revealed reality lying at the basis of and agreeing with an appearance.' In other words—they match," Holly shared. "They must match, so as not to be false."

Holly looked gently into Steve's eyes and continued. "I think you have never fully embraced your worth, Steve. Or the fact that God finds you incredibly valuable. You teach others, but when it comes to yourself you are stuck on one side of the *altheia* definition—believing it with your head and for others—but not on the other side of believing it with your heart and for yourself. It's not matching up. Your head and heart are not in agreement. Maybe it's time to close the gap."

Steve was floored by all of Holly's words. That night it was Steve who was tossing and turning. He began praying earnestly, asking God to help him believe deeply that he was valuable. He knew intellectually that God found him valuable, but he didn't feel it for himself. It would take time and many prayers.

He also was able to see how his intentional pausing exercise would need to include the times when he felt the emotions of being undeserving. He would rethink this in light of who God is and how God sees him, not how others see him or even how he sees himself.

Interestingly, Steve had just been reading a book by author Dane Ortlund, *Deeper,* that spoke about the human tendency to live into others' value of us—even when we say we believe that God values us. *This is what*

Holly is trying to say, Steve thought to himself. He pulled out the book and read Ortlund's words carefully and thoughtfully:

> What we tend to do is walk through life amassing a sense of who we are as an aggregate of what we think everyone else thinks of us. We walk along, building a sense of self through all the feedback pinging at us. We don't even realize we're doing it. And when others are critical, or snub us, or ignore us, or ridicule us, that builds our sense of who we are. It inevitably shapes us. And so we must constantly hold the gospel before our eyes. And as the gospel becomes real to us, the need for human approval loses its vice-like grip on our hearts, because we are no longer putting our heads down on our pillows at night medicating our sense of worth with human approval.[1]

Since Steve never felt celebrated, he felt undeserving of it. He was comfortable celebrating others but was now recognizing that it was okay to celebrate his own life and accomplishments. These emotions, as Holly mentioned earlier, were safe for him to embrace. *The next time the professor or a waitress remarks about me and Holly being a couple, I will say, "We are blessed,"* Steve thought to himself. This would be a great start

---

1   Dane Ortlund, *Deeper*, (Crossway, 2021), p. 98.

to overcoming his habit of downplaying himself and feeling undeserving.

❦

As Steve pondered all these thoughts and how the belt of truth is so critical to counter self-loathing, it stirred the pastor's heart in him. *God loves the person inside not because of any advantages on the outside*, Steve thought to himself.

Inspired, Steve grabbed a pen to add the following thoughts to his intentional pausing paper:

Imagine taking away the layers of your identity, one by one. First, take away appearance, then talents, then position, then preferences, then possessions, then political beliefs, then connections, then cultural influences, then circumstances, then status.

What's left? Who are we after all that is removed?

This is who matters to God, not all the other things. God loves and cherishes the person inside, the simple you, who is born with nothing and dies with nothing. God wants to reach that person with a truth that anchors the mind (and heart).

5

Jan

Jan's affections were instantly set on John. He was handsome, with dark wavy hair and piercing blue eyes. When the teacher asked the students to share what inspired them to take his class, Jan couldn't help but notice that another classmate named Noel caught John's interest. Her answer seemed dull to Jan; she was annoyed that John perked up over it.

What does she have that I don't? Jan thought.

This feeling wasn't uncommon for Jan, and it always caused her to ramp up her game. For instance, when John cracked jokes during lectures to make Noel smile, Jan would laugh generously to draw the attention her direction.

Jan carefully selected outfits that were eye-catching.

Whenever John was in the vicinity, she would position herself within his view. These things were all deliberate. The less interest John showed, the more motivated Jan became. Although Jan didn't really know Noel, she saw her as a threat. Jan wanted the spotlight, but it kept falling on Noel as far as John was concerned.

Noel didn't notice the extra measures Jan was taking toward John, because heads generally turned Jan's direction when Jan was around. Noel did notice, however, that Jan exuded confidence, something Noel wished she had.

Jan looked for cracks in Noel, things that would give her the advantage. For instance, Jan noticed that Noel always wore the same shoes. This motivated Jan to wear an array of footwear reflecting style, designer brand, and privilege. When the professor asked questions, Jan observed that Noel would give short, simple answers. In contrast, Jan showcased her ability of expression by answering questions with lengthy eloquence. On another occasion, Noel appeared stoic. This prompted Jan to express sympathy-grabbing vulnerability for the purpose of winning favor. All these things were attempts to outdo Noel.

When Jan missed class one day due to a twenty-four-hour stomach bug, she asked John for the session notes. John shared that he, too, had been sick and absent that day. Jan immediately recognized an opportunity, and she asked John for Noel's cell number for notes.

John passed Noel's number on without hesitation.

That evening Jan texted Noel. "Hi Noel, this is Jan Foley. John gave me your cell number. I hope you don't mind."

Jan was hoping this text might give Noel the impression that she knew John on a personal level. And it did. She didn't really care if Noel responded or not. This was simply a tactic to unsettle Noel.

"What can I help with, Jan?"

"I missed Tuesday's class. John told me you might have some notes that I could use to study from," Jan responded.

When Jan went to class the next day, she could see from Noel's aloof demeaner toward John that she had succeeded in causing discord. But what surprised Jan was that Noel was displaying aloofness instead of visible insecurity.

Jan waited a few weeks before asking John if they could study together off campus. Finally, she approached the subject. "John, would you be interested in studying together after class?"

John hesitated. He had sensed Jan's intensity for some time and was still raw from Noel's sudden and unexplained detachment. "Sorry, Jan, I was planning on studying with my friend Steve," John said apologetically.

He also added, "I am coming out of a relationship and am looking forward to some guy-time." John was signaling to Jan that he was not available, or at least his heart wasn't. Jan felt a short-lived pang of guilt. She knew John was talking about Noel and that she had played a role in Noel's shutting John out.

Jan hated this about herself but at the same time couldn't seem to help it. She leaned on her beauty and confidence to navigate what she perceived as obstacles. And when she wanted something, she went after it without considering the collateral damage she might cause.

In this case, it was Noel and John's relationship. Disappointed that her efforts didn't win John and mulling over the outcome of her actions, Jan had another idea. It was John's mention of "guy-time" that inspired her.

Jan reached out to her friend Holly. "How about some girl-time—Chinese food and a movie in my dorm Friday?"

"That sounds great," Holly replied. "I could really use the break."

When Friday arrived, Jan laid out a choice selection of food from the best Chinese delivery restaurant in town. Jan's favorite was the moo goo gai pan; Holly's was sesame chicken. Jan ordered spring rolls, fried rice, and dumplings as sides. All of it was delicious.

Jan was ready to move forward with her idea—so before starting a movie, she initiated a conversation with Holly.

"It didn't work out with John and I getting together," Jan said.

Holly knew Jan had a big heart for John.

"I really think you two would hit it off, Holly," Jan added casually.

"What? No, Jan, I would not get close to John while you still care for him."

"You would be doing me a favor," Jan said confidently. "It would take him off my radar." She laughed. "He and I are incompatible—plus, you and he are perfect."

Jan said these things knowing that Holly had a similar personality to Noel. Deep down inside, Jan felt like she would still be winning if she could win John over to someone other than Noel, someone she liked and was close to.

Monday came, and Jan was still in planning mode ready to make the connection. When she saw John, she asked if he had a minute to talk.

"Sure," John said curiously.

"I have a friend named Holly who would be perfect for you. She reminds me a lot of a girl in our class named Noel," Jan said winsomely.

This intrigued John. Just the thought of spending time with anyone who was like Noel lifted his broken heart. Jan could see this in his eyes.

Holly didn't share the same classes as Noel or John—only John's friend Steve. Holly was a psychology major like Steve. Steve thought Holly was a lovely person. And when Holly started dating John, he was happy for John. Being a great wingman, Steve thought to himself, *Holly deserves a good guy like John.*

Steve was unaware that it was Jan who initiated the connection between Holly and John. After all, Jan simply put the idea in both of their minds, and it happened on its own.

For the most part it was a wonderful match. They were similar people with common interests. Except for one notable difference: food. John had a refined palate, and Holly was a biscuits and gravy kind of girl. But this didn't interfere with their enjoyable interactions.

Holly's knowledge of mental health interested John, and John's comical personality delighted Holly, although she had noticed moments of deep sadness that would come over him. Holly shared this with Jan, but Jan was careful never to mention Noel. Instead, she redirected Holly to use her art of encouragement to help John through his sadness.

All seemed to be working out as planned. That is, until Jan's phone chimed with an incoming text from Noel.

PART 2

(Jan's emotions)

Jan did not know how to respond when Noel sent a text after Christmas break.

The text read, "Hi Jan, this is Noel. I have your number from the time you texted me for study notes. You came to my mind over the holidays, and I wondered if we could connect for coffee."

Perplexed, Jan took a few hours to reply.

"Sure, that sounds fun." But Jan didn't mean it. She was suspicious, curious what Noel was up to.

This is how Jan's mind worked, always calculating and positioning. She was either maneuvering to get something or evaluating what other people were trying to get from her. Noel's request threw her. Jan didn't perceive Noel to be cunning. *Maybe she is going to confront me about John*, Jan thought to herself.

Jan began formulating plausible excuses in her mind for her role in Noel and John's relationship downfall. She wanted to be ready should the subject surface. This way Jan could spin or shape it so it didn't reflect poorly on her. She was good at influencing favor in her direction.

Jan's early years had been different. Circumstances were not easy, and she did not have this skill of swaying favor. Jan was the scapegoat more than she would like to remember. She never considered herself pretty as a child. In fact, she considered herself extremely ugly. She hated seeing pictures of when she was young. It seemed to her as if kids and adults alike picked on her mercilessly. It was at this time in her life that she drew close to God. In her mind He was her only friend.

As Jan got a bit older, she began learning how to navigate people who treated her poorly. She hated the feelings of worthlessness that would overtake her when this occurred, so deflecting became a tool for emotional survival. But this meant Jan was always on alert. Looking for ways to sway mean people other directions. The goal was to cease being the scapegoat.

After Jan went through her teenage years, a remarkable change happened with her appearance. Her braces came off, contacts went in, and Jan emerged as a one-of-a-kind beauty. And it was no ordinary beauty; it was jaw-dropping. Her once mean-spirited enemies were now pursuing her like she was a Venus.

Jan became empowered in a new way, and she liked it.

In Jan's mind she had finally made it. Doors opened and oppression lifted. Still, underneath her confident beauty Jan struggled. There was always a pressing internal drive to maintain favor. She couldn't bear feeling overlooked; it brought back old feelings of worthlessness. She worked hard at being number one in the lives of people who mattered to her. Feeling second was unbearably painful. It was the pain of her childhood trauma.

These emotions compelled her to become the gatekeeper in all her relationships. That meant you would have to go through her to have any kind of connection with people who were important to her. She was constantly assessing ranking within this context.

This is what happened in her heart concerning John. She tried to gain favor from him over Noel, but it wasn't happening. This made Jan pursue harder. Not so much because she liked John, which she did, but because she didn't want to experience the pain of rejection.

When she saw that her efforts still weren't working—even after causing conflict between Noel and John—she devised another plan that would make her a gatekeeper of sorts over John. That plan included Holly. Bringing Holly into John's life would close the gate on Noel.

Jan was unaware of how her past emotional experiences were influencing her present actions. They had developed into an automatic form of self-protection. In other words, Jan had cultivated methods of manipulation to shield herself from pain.

Because Jan had not worked through her past pain in healthy ways, she was never at rest or at peace with herself. Her life was made up of continual crafted presentations to feel safe. But in the process she became unsafe, and many people felt that sense of danger around her. Being her friend might land someone in her version of a narrative that made her look good and them look bad.

Noel knew she was taking a chance reaching out to Jan. But she also knew what it was like to allow evaluations of her own worth to play out in self-sabotaging ways. She decided not to inquire whether Jan and John were in a relationship.

Noel's heart went out to Jan. She saw something in her, a fragility under the confidence and beauty. She had noticed on several occasions a pained look come over Jan's face when students in class were praised by the professor. This was usually followed later by Jan pointing out a flaw in that person. Noel perceived this to come from feeling unimportant. In Noel's mind Jan's presentation was always on overdrive for this reason.

Noel's conversations with the counselor at Christmas had stirred this thought. Particularly the verse Philippians 2:3, when the counselor had shared about being equal—that is, one person not being more valuable than another. She considered how Jan might be putting up a front because she felt insignificant, possibly a secret kind of self-loathing where she was using her beauty as a cover-up. Noel wanted to see Jan through the eyes of mercy.

Noel made sure to talk with her counselor before reaching out to Jan. And her counselor was careful to suggest several boundaries that might be helpful to put in place.

"A boundary does not mean no connection," she assured Noel, even commending her kindness toward Jan. "Sometimes a boundary is simply a defining line that keeps us safe with certain people. In other words, with someone like Jan you can make the decision ahead of time not to reveal your vulnerabilities."

Noel tucked this away in her heart.

Noel was looking forward to having coffee with Jan but was also nervous. Based on her conversations with her counselor, Noel solidified a personal boundary in her mind that she would not talk about John or herself in a personal way. This would be a coffee get-together based on goodwill with no expectations. Noel prayed for both safety and wisdom.

PART 3

(The lens of mercy)

Jan suggested meeting for coffee at a restaurant called Eden's Eatery twenty-five minutes from the campus. She wanted to avoid meeting locally for fear that John, Steve, or Holly might see her and Noel together. She wasn't about do that, at least not until she figured out what Noel was up to.

The restaurant Jan picked boasted of fruits and fresh garden greens, and the coffee was advertised as organic. Noel liked this idea; healthy food was always a good option.

Noel prayed the entire drive that God would give her wisdom and protection. She was feeling nervous about stepping out of her comfort zone. Noel had always admired Jan's confidence and poise, even marveling at how Jan would burst out laughing at John's wisecracks during class. Noel wished she could do the same without feeling shame. Instead, she worried about looking silly, but Jan never looked silly, she looked free. Or was she?

Noel was grateful that she arrived first. She asked the hostess for the high-top table near the window. *People-watching might take the edge off*, Noel thought to herself.

Jan arrived and made her way to the table and sat confidently on the stool. Noel couldn't help but notice other customers' eyes drawn to Jan's great beauty. Jan's trendy outfit made her look like she'd stepped off the pages of a magazine.

Noel smiled. "It seems you have some fans."

"Ehh," Jan replied in a polite and unimpressed manner. "How was your Christmas, Noel?" she said, changing the subject.

"Very good, lots of 'new,' " Noel replied. Jan looked puzzled; Noel's words sounded cryptic. Suddenly Jan became distracted, shifting her focus to a dog outside the window wearing a red sweater. Jan chuckled. Noel was glad she had picked the table near the window for this reason.

"I'm curious, Noel, what prompted you wanting to meet for coffee?"

"Speaking of coffee," Noel interjected, "let's place an order. Order anything you like—my treat."

"I think I'll try the chocolate avocado mousse and a cinnamon latte," Jan said, thanking Noel for her offer to treat.

"Okay," Noel began, "during Christmas break I thought about you."

Jan's eyes filled with curiosity.

"You always seem so put-together." Noel paused and continued choosing her words carefully. "I am in therapy right now to understand myself better."

Noel didn't mind sharing this. It wasn't personal—if anything, seeing a therapist was trendy these days.

"Also, the humanities class we are taking is about understanding culture and what makes people who they are," Noel shared.

Jan still looked curious.

Noel continued, "I want to find out what has shaped your confidence in life. More specifically, I love that you laugh freely and enjoy life."

This is not what Jan had expected, not at all.

Noel saw this get-together as an opportunity to discover what makes a confident person tick. Plus, she wanted to see the good in Jan. Those characteristics in Jan, carrying herself with aplomb and laughing with carefree abandon, were something Noel admired.

Putting her coffee cup down and looking serious, Noel asked, "Do you mind sharing what you can, no pressure—what has made you so self-assured?"

This conversation, the meeting, all of it caught Jan off guard; it was disarming. Jan took a deep breath. She was geared up for damage control, the fallout of her own actions of manipulation, that is. She looked at Noel to size her up. She saw kindness and sincerity in her eyes.

"I haven't always been confident," Jan said with a half smile.

"Really?" Noel replied. "You weren't born with it, then?"

"Well, I think laughter comes naturally to me," Jan asserted. "I enjoy humor. Most of my family members are funny."

Noel listened intently as Jan continued. "During difficult times in my young life, humor was a tonic I was drawn to. They say that laughter decreases stress hormones, you know."

"I did not know that, but it makes sense," Noel responded.

Noel had a fleeting thought about suppressing her laughter over the years and the possibility of that building up stress hormones. She did not share this thought with Jan; it was too vulnerable. But she did mentally file it away to share with her counselor later.

"Confidence came harder to me. I think I have a fighting spirit, so when I was going through difficulties growing up, I fought for confidence," Jan explained. "Does that make sense?"

"Gosh, it really does," Noel replied.

Jan sensed that this conversation went deeper than Noel was letting on. This was one of Jan's strengths—assessing situations. Her heart softened, and she asked Noel why she was so interested in how confidence is shaped.

"Like I mentioned earlier, I am seeing a therapist."

"Yes, you said."

"Confidence is something I am working on person-ally. And I have always admired yours." Noel wondered as the words came out of her mouth if she was bordering on vulnerability.

The question Noel would ask herself when trying to evaluate was, *Do I mind if what I am saying is shared outside of this conversation?* She felt safe.

Jan chimed in. "Well, I admire your determination to work on it. It looks like you might have a fighting spirit too." Noel smiled. "Just be careful," Jan added. "Confidence can go too far, and you can find yourself doing, and being, something you really don't want to do or be."

Wow, Jan is being vulnerable, Noel thought to herself.

For the next hour they chatted about the dynamics of confidence. The good and the ugly, but nothing personal. There was lots of laughter. A fun, lively personality was something they had in common, even though Noel had squelched hers for years. Heads were turning, but not at Jan's beauty. This time it was to see where the hearty roaring was coming from. It felt good for Noel to laugh, and it came easy with Jan.

Jan felt a connection with Noel, a sincerity she admired. This meeting had gone differently than Jan expected. She was pleasantly surprised and refreshed by Noel's personality. And Noel was happy to see Jan through the eyes she knew God saw her through. Noel knew there was more to Jan's story. Her statement of how confidence can go too far revealed to Noel that Jan had some of her own self-loathing going on.

And that is exactly what happened on Jan's drive home. She agonized at the horrible person she thought she was. She felt sick to her stomach thinking about it. Her previous schemes and jealousy of Noel, set against the kind and genuine person she connected with today, made this recognition even clearer than usual. She could barely stand herself, and it weighed heavy on her.

Noel left the restaurant feeling glad that she'd stepped out of her comfort zone and reached out. She knew Jan had a reputation at school for putting people down and could be a difficult adversary, so she stuck to her boundary of not disclosing vulnerabilities. But Noel also held on to what she learned in counseling—that *mercy* is compassionate and kindly forbearance shown toward an adversary.

This thought gave her courage, especially when she considered how Jesus treated people. He always loved them right where they were and at the same time saw all they could be. The truth was that Noel had a lot to learn herself. That day she learned quite a bit talking with Jan, and she was grateful.

6

(Noel, John, Holly, Steve & Jan)

The room was beautifully arrayed with white roses and daisies. It took Noel's breath away as she walked through the chapel doors. Holly and Steve's wedding venue looked like a garden fairy tale.

In the vestibule to the right was a large engagement poster of Holly and Steve in front of their favorite diner, The Farmer and the Grill. Under the poster stood a small stand that held the Bible verse Miss Vera had given Steve. Off to the side was a napkin with James 2:5 scribbled on it: *Has not God chosen those who are poor in the eyes of the world to be rich in faith?* Next to this were the bells that had fallen from the diner door the day Holly and Steve knew their hearts were meant for each other. Noel studied these items and wondered what their meanings had been in the lives of this sweet couple.

It was hard for Noel to believe that Steve was getting married. She was happy for him, though. He had always been there for her, and she was glad to be there for him on his special day. Steve and Noel's families had lived next door to each other over the years, and both were in attendance.

As Noel made her way into the seating area, Noel's mom waved her over.

Holly and Steve's friends filled the pews as the time of the ceremony drew closer. Noel smiled at the professor who was beaming with delight at the front of the room. It was Professor Stan. *I had no idea he was the officiating minister*, Noel thought to herself.

The music began to play as the groom and his groomsmen emerged from the side door. Noel's heart leaped when she saw John. He was Steve's best man and was dressed in a pale yellow tux. *Keep it together*, Noel said to herself as she began to feel a sense of sadness and mounting anxiety. *Deep breaths, deep breaths.* Noel had learned some self-regulation techniques from her counselor and knew this was a good time to employ them.

"Take notice of your senses; this will ground you," her counselor had told her. First, Noel took notice of the feel of the floor beneath her feet. She tapped her toe to make sure she could feel the texture. It was wood.

Then, taking in a deep breath, she smelled the fragrance of the roses attached to the pew. Finally, Noel listened to the soft, gentle flow of the music.

Noel's counselor had added one more important part to the self-regulating process—a faith-regulating part of the practice. "After taking notice of your senses, thank God for three things in your life that are good." This instruction came from one of the counselor's most reorienting verses, 1 Thessalonians 5:18, "Give thanks in all circumstances."

Silently, in a short prayer Noel thanked God for Steve being such a wonderful friend her whole life, and for her counselor who was helping her work through self-loathing. And finally, she thanked God for John, who was part of bringing about the recognition of the need for change in her life.

Noel's mom squeezed her hand as Noel steadied herself. She was glad her parents were there. She thanked God for that too.

Steve's parents and Holly's mom were escorted in and seated in the front row.

As the music continued, a parade of bridesmaids walked down the center aisle. Jan, who was Holly's maid of honor, looked absolutely stunning in a full-length yellow chiffon dress. Noel couldn't help noticing John's eyes drawn to Jan's radiant beauty. Her heart ached, but she had already determined to be happy for John, whoever he chose to be in a relationship with.

A darling ring bearer and flower girl appeared, tossing fistfuls of petals into the crowd. They seemed eager to outdo each other, and the delighted audience responded with "Oohs" and "Ahhs."

The music turned dramatic as the bride, escorted by her father, appeared in the doorway. All eyes watched as Holly made her way down the aisle toward Steve. She was wearing a simple, flowing white gown. Noel glanced back at Steve to see his eyes glistening with tear-filled love.

❧

"What a beautiful wedding," one of Steve's friends said at the reception table where Noel was sitting. Everyone seated chimed in their agreement. Noel was distracted as she studied the bridal party table. They were laughing and having fun. Noel was glad to see John happy.

Noel turned her attention back to her table. The food was delicious: glazed orange chicken, buttered baby carrots, and a strawberry Brie salad. Noel was surprised that she didn't know anyone at her table.

The handsome young man sitting next to her introduced himself. "Hi, I'm Mateo." Mateo was tan and toned with a charming smile.

"I'm Noel, it's nice to meet you. How do you know Steve?" Noel asked curiously.

"We're both psychology majors. I know both Holly and Steve from campus. How about you?"

"I grew up next door to Steve."

"Ah, Steve told me about you. He said I needed to meet you."

Noel looked a little caught off guard.

"He said you were one of his favorite people in the world."

A smile came over Noel's face.

The sound of a knife tapping on a glass filled the room. It was time for the wedding toasts. John was standing, waiting for the table conversations to quiet.

"Well," John said, "I'm not sure how many of you know the whole story."

There were chuckles all around the room. But Noel did not know the whole story.

"I connected with Steve at a very difficult season. It was during a time someone I cared deeply for stepped out of my life. Steve was there for me like a brother." John's eyes started to water.

"A better friend no man has ever had," John said while looking at Steve.

Noel's eyes widened as he continued.

"Then I became friends with the lovely Holly Madison, only to have Steve boot me out of her life."

The room laughed and cheered.

"They are both very dear friends to me, and I couldn't be happier that they are together. There isn't a more perfect match in the world of two beautiful hearts!"

Next, Jan stood to make her toast. "If we are doing

confessions, here's mine."

Jan, being caught up in the momentum, went on. "What many of you don't know is that I am the one who set up John and Holly in the first place."

The crowd burst into laughter.

"I am glad that my plans didn't work out. And that my dear friend Holly met the love of her life regardless of my meddling. God has His ways of bringing the right people together. In both marriage . . . and friendship." Jan's eyes glanced Noel's direction.

Then, putting her focus back on Holly and Steve, Jan continued. "Here's to the most loving, meant-to-be couple in the world!"

PART 2

(Emotions of change)

Something special was happening in the reception hall. Noel sensed change. There was a shift in Jan's countenance. It was slight, but noticeable. Noel could hear it in her voice during the toast. *Could something be happening in Jan's heart?*

Noel reminded herself of a thought her counselor had shared, "Change doesn't happen all at once; it takes time." She had cautioned Noel not to give in to the pressure of Christian culture that makes people think change happens instantly. "This is a setup for failure," her counselor warned. These words were comforting. Noel realized growth takes time, and not just for her but for everyone. One baby step at a time.

Music began playing as the announcer invited Steve and Holly onto the dance floor. They gazed into each other's eyes as they glided with grace across the dark surface of the room's beautiful wood floor. All eyes were locked in entrancement.

Noel felt a hand touch her shoulder. She turned to

see Jan standing with a smile on her face. "Hi, Noel."

Noel stood and hugged her. "You did a beautiful job with your toast," Noel said.

"Thank you," Jan replied. "Listen, do you have a minute to talk?" Jan's face looked vulnerable.

"Of course."

Jan led the way to a seating area in the front of the hall. In those few moments of walking to the lobby, Noel wondered what was so important that Jan would step away from the reception. Noel said a short silent prayer. *Lord, please give me wisdom for whatever is bothering Jan.*

They both sat down, and Jan sighed deeply. "Noel, do you remember last year when you and John Ryan were hanging out off campus to study?"

"Yes," Noel replied curiously. Just hearing John's name caused Noel anxiety. She knew she needed to ground herself so she could focus on what Jan was about to say. And it needed to be quick. This self-regulation happened in a matter of seconds. *Baby steps*, Noel thought to herself.

Jan continued. "I need to confess something to you."

"Okay," Noel said hesitantly.

"I sent you that text for study notes last year hoping you would think John and I were closer than we really were."

Noel was quiet.

"I am so sorry, Noel—I knew John had a heart for you, and I tried to interfere."

Noel's eyes filled with tears.

It all started to make sense in Noel's mind. But she found herself without words, unable to respond. On the one hand, Noel felt brokenhearted that Jan played a significant role in her losing John. But on the other, she was grateful that the heartache had led her to some important recognition of her own role in the relationship's downfall—as well as other areas of her life.

The verse Romans 8:28 came to Noel's mind: "We know that in all things God works for the good of those who love him, who have been called according to his purpose."

"Can you forgive me, Noel?" Jan asked in a regretful tone.

Noel remained quiet as more thoughts entered her mind. She remembered what caused her to reach out to Jan in the first place. She had considered how Jan might be putting up a front because of feelings of insignificance, possibly a secret kind of self-loathing where she was using her beauty as a cover-up. Noel had wanted to see Jan through the eyes of mercy.

"Of course," Noel said with a weak but genuine smile. Jan burst into tears and embraced her. Jan was grateful. She had really grown to care for Noel. She trusted her. Noel was a kind figure in her life. God's hand of grace extended. And Noel truly appreciated Jan and valued her. They had become friends—unexpected friends.

This didn't mean Noel trusted Jan; she knew she still needed to keep boundaries in place. The counselor had told Noel that trust needs to be earned over time. Boundaries are adaptable as trust is built. But in some cases, an emotional guardrail must stay in place indefinitely. Nevertheless, Noel knew in her heart that it was a very big deal that Jan had made herself vulnerable and confessed.

"Hi, Noel." A deep voice spoke from behind where Jan and Noel were sitting. They looked up to see Mateo standing tall and handsome. His suit was trendy and expensive-looking. "Would you care to dance?" Mateo said with a gleaming smile.

"Yes," Noel said promptly, standing and feeling like this would be a good time to exit the conversation with Jan.

She needed to sort out her own feelings over what Jan shared, and that she would have to do privately with her counselor.

A few minutes into her dance with Mateo, out of the corner of her eye Noel saw John dancing with Jan. There was no question that they made a beautiful couple.

Was Jan's confession a way to get to John? Noel wondered.

This thought quickly entered her mind, and then another.

Did John tell her she needed make things right with me before they move forward? Wait a minute! I'm agonizing.

Noel remembered the counselor's recommendation to allow the intensity of the emotions serve as an alert system.

Noel could feel her heart racing. Trying to calm down, she began her self-regulating techniques while dancing. But they were not helping. As hard as Noel tried to ground herself, a flood of sadness swept over her. *Why isn't it working?* she wondered. And with that thought, tears began to well up in her eyes.

Mateo, concerned, asked, "Are you okay?"

Noel mustered up a stoic, "Yes, just happy tears for the bride and groom," before excusing herself to the restroom.

This was Noel's best attempt to not allow her emotions to take control and cause a scene. After all, she really was happy for the bride and groom. Grabbing her purse from the table, she whisked herself away.

Beside the restroom, Noel saw another door labeled Sitting Room. She slipped in quietly and locked the door behind her.

It was lovely space with an oversized cozy floral couch. She was happy to have found herself there. She said a quick prayer. *Thank you, Lord, for this perfect place to regroup.* She pulled out her phone and dialed her counselor. When her counselor picked up, Noel shared all the details going on with her emotions at the wedding and reception.

PART 3

(The lens of patience)

"I just don't understand why the self-regulating and grounding techniques didn't work!" Noel told her counselor. "I'd been doing so well up until then." She let out a big sigh of disappointment as her tears flowed.

"Self-regulating and grounding techniques are not magic, Noel. They are just tools to allow space for healthy thoughts to enter our minds," the counselor said.

Noel was quiet. She was relying on these techniques, and they had let her down.

"Do you remember our conversation on self-loathing in terms of a storm system brewing?" the counselor asked.

"Yes," Noel said.

"We characterized all these swirling emotions in terms of weight—like the weight described in the original meaning of Hebrews 12, a mass or bulging load." The counselor continued, "Your day was packed with swirling massive emotional weight."

"Yes, it felt very heavy and very chaotic," Noel exclaimed.

"You are not always going to bear up under the

weight of pain, Noel. Your humanity is real. This is where you will need to learn to be patient with yourself. Just as God is patient with you. We are all a work in progress, and it's in our weakness that we lean into Him. It's okay not to be okay."

The counselor's words were comforting to Noel. She had been putting too much pressure on herself and the grounding techniques.

"Why can't I stop crying?" Noel asked.

"When Jan sat you down to confess—those pressurized emotions of losing John came rushing in. You tried to prop up your resilience with new thoughts about how Jan has changed. But the prop soon collapsed when you saw Jan dancing with John."

"Oh my gosh," Noel said. "That's exactly what happened."

"Mateo's invitation to dance was a welcome escape, but not even that was able to bear up under that pain of grief," the counselor shared.

"Grief?"

"Depths of grief are different for everyone. Have you ever heard the saying after someone dies—that tears are a tribute to the depth of your love?"

"Yes, I've always loved that saying because it puts honor in tears," Noel replied.

"It's the same with your grief over John, Noel. It runs very deep. That is part of the heaviness you are feeling today."

Noel was quiet. She was grateful she had called her counselor. In fact, as she thought back, she couldn't help but marvel at how God had watched over her in various ways. Steve was a constant, stable presence in her life, and he was the one who had led her to the counselor who was an extension of this. Even this small sitting room was a blessing. The freedom to express her pain in a safe space became a grounding moment, enough to get her on her feet and back into the wedding reception.

As Noel scanned the room, she saw John in deep conversation with Steve at a small table. As she glanced toward the center of the room, she noticed Jan on the dance floor. She looked happy. Noel was relieved not to see her in John's arms. Then looking to the left, Noel noticed her parents sitting with Steve's parents enjoying the festivities, and she joined their table. *If I can just get through this day*, Noel thought to herself.

It wasn't long before Mateo pulled up a chair next to Noel. "I wanted to check on you, Noel. Are you okay?"

"Yes, thank you, Mateo." Noel had no intention of divulging any personal information. But it was nice that he checked on her.

"Also, I wanted to ask you—who was that gorgeous creature you were sitting with when I asked you to dance?" Mateo gushed.

Fantastic, just what I needed to hear, Noel thought to herself.

"That's Jan Foley, and yes, she is very beautiful," Noel said.

Mateo's eyes told Noel he was enamored. "Do you know if she is seeing anyone?"

"I think she is seeing John Ryan," Noel stated as nonchalantly as she could muster.

"That's too bad. I mean—for me." Mateo chuckled. Noel managed a weak smile.

Noel glanced over to where she last saw John sitting with Steve. They were still there. *What is so important that Steve would take so much time away from his new bride?* Noel wondered. According to John's toast, he and Steve had grown very close. *Maybe they are talking about Jan's confession to me, and Steve is giving him his blessing to pursue her now.*

This thought processing caused her to remember the flashing yellow warning sign of impending self-loathing. *I think it's time for me to leave,* Noel said to herself.

Hugging her parents goodbye, Noel headed toward a nearby hallway. She didn't want to get stopped, so she increased her pace to the exit. With every step her heart pounded harder. *I'm almost out of the building.*

Reaching for the door handle brought instant relief. But just then a hand reached over hers and held the door open. It was John. "Are you leaving without saying goodbye?"

Noel, shocked, looked at John as if he were an enemy.

This was her old habit of aloofness kicking in as a

form of self-protection. She really didn't want to hear about how it was going between him and Jan. She had had enough *confessions* for the day.

"Bye, John," she said as she kept walking toward her car.

John stood there for a few seconds with his hands on his hips, assessing Noel's determined pace. "Oh, I get it—you're ghosting me again."

With that, Noel spun around and said, "What!?"

"I will say this—I have never seen a more beautiful ghost!" John said with charm and a smile.

"Are you trying to be cryptic?" Noel said with a glare.

"On the contrary, Noel, I am trying to be clear. Sometimes there is only one shot with a fleeing ghost. Especially one so beautiful and fast."

Remembering John's warmth and sense of humor softened Noel enough to stand still.

"I've missed you," John said, stepping closer. The stars were glistening above them. "I didn't realize a ghost could look so stunning in the moonlight," he said softly with love in his eyes.

All at once Noel was gripped with recognition. Standing there looking into John's eyes, Noel made the instant connection to how a year ago, she was mistakenly convinced that John had chosen Jan over her. And she was about to do it again.

Or was she?